USBORNE FIRST READING

The
Old Woman
who lived in a
Shoe

Retold by Russell Punter
Illustrated by Joelle Dreidemy

USBORNE FIRST READING

Brer
Rabbit
and the
Blackberry Bush

Retold by
Louie Stowell
Illustrated by
Eva Muszynski

USBORNE FIRST READING

How
Elephants lost
their Wings

Retold by
Lesley Sims
Illustrated by Katie Lovell

USBORNE FIRST READING

The
Chilly Little
Penguin

Russell Punter
Illustrated by Stephen Gulbis

Brer Rabbit Down the Well

Retold by Louie Stowell

Illustrated by
Eva Muszynski

Reading consultant: Alison Kelly
Roehampton University

This is a
story about
Brer Rabbit,

Brer Fox

and a deep,
dark well.

Brer Rabbit was
running very fast.

Brer Fox was
chasing him.

"I'm going to eat you up," growled Brer Fox.

Brer Rabbit ran faster.

He came to a deep, dark well.

"I can hide here," he thought.

He jumped into the
bucket.

But the bucket started
to fall.

The
bucket
fell...

and
fell.

Splosh!
"How will I get out?"
thought Brer Rabbit.

"Found you!" said a voice from above.

It was Brer Fox.

"You can't hide from me," he growled.

"I'm not hiding,"
said Brer Rabbit.

"I'm fishing."

"There are some
huge fish here."

Splash!
He made a splashing
sound with his paw.

13

"I've got one," cried
Brer Rabbit.

Splash!

"And another!"

"Come down here," he added. "Or there won't be any left."

Brer Fox loved fish.

He forgot about eating
Brer Rabbit.

He turned the handle.
The bucket came up.

Brer Rabbit hopped
out. Brer Fox got in.

17

And Brer
Fox fell...

and
fell...

and
fell.

Splash!

Brer Rabbit looked
down at Brer Fox.

He laughed.

"Where are the fish?" growled Brer Fox.

"In the river," said Brer Rabbit.

"I'm going to catch some right now."

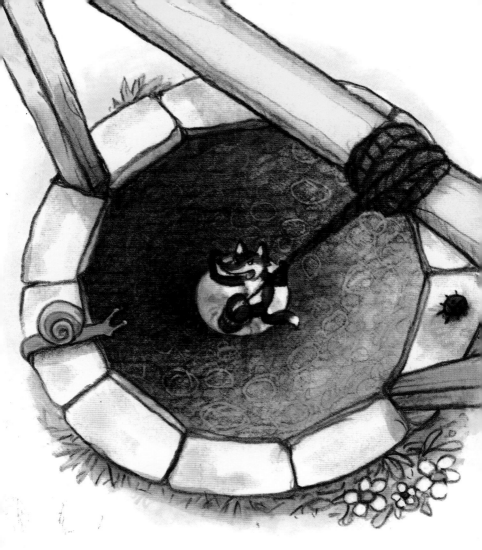

Brer Fox howled. "You
tricked me!"

But Brer
Rabbit had
walked away.

HELP!

It took Brer Fox
a *very* long time
to climb out.

25

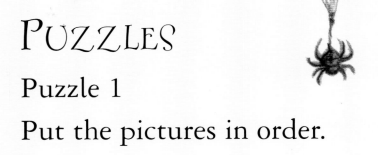

Puzzles

Puzzle 1

Put the pictures in order.

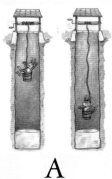

A

B

C

D

E

F

Puzzle 2
Find these things in
the picture:
owl   hedgehog   sheep
snail   Brer Rabbit   spider

Puzzle 3
Choose the best speech bubble for each picture.

Answers to puzzles

Puzzle 1

E A F D C B

Puzzle 2

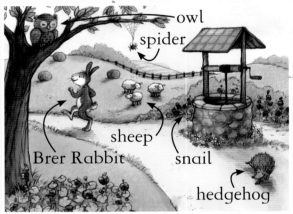

owl
spider
Brer Rabbit
sheep
snail
hedgehog

Puzzle 3

"I'm running."   "It's wet."   "I'm hiding."

About this story

In the 19th century, an American named Joel Chandler Harris wrote a series of tales about Brer Rabbit, Brer Fox, and other animal characters. But he didn't entirely make them up. A lot of his stories are very similar to earlier African and Cherokee legends.

Designed by Caroline Spatz
Series designer: Russell Punter
Series editor: Lesley Sims

First published in 2009 by Usborne Publishing Ltd., Usborne House,
83-85 Saffron Hill, London EC1N 8RT, England. www.usborne.com
Copyright © 2009 Usborne Publishing Ltd.